Harriet and George's

CHRISTMAS TREAT

Harriet and George's CHRISTMAS TREAT

Nancy ★ Carlson

SCHOLASTIC INC.
New York Toronto London Auckland Sydney
Mexico City New Delhi Hong Kong Buenos Aires

ISBN 0-439-46769-1

12 11 10 9 8 7 6 5 4 3 2 1   2 3 4 5 6 7/0

Printed in the U.S.A.   24

First Scholastic printing, November 2002

To my friends at the Nutcracker Sweet, Barbie, Debbie, and Noni!

Thank you for all your wonderful work with children!!!

I still miss the mother's tea!

It was almost Christmas.

Harriet and George were going shopping when they saw Ms. Hoozit leave the grocery store.

"Hi, Ms. Hoozit," said Harriet.
"Hi, kids," said Ms. Hoozit. "No time to talk. I'm off to do my holiday baking. Now be sure to stop over later for a Christmas treat!" Ms. Hoozit rushed away.

"Oh, no! Ms. Hoozit is going home to bake!" said George.
"That can mean only one thing!" said Harriet.

"Ms. Hoozit is making fruitcake!"

"Remember last year when Ms. Hoozit made us try a piece right in front of her?" said George.

"Yuck! It tasted awful," said Harriet.
"And I almost broke a tooth."

"Remember when you dropped Ms. Hoozit's fruitcake on your foot?" said Harriet.
"Ouch! That really hurt!" said George.

"But it worked great for cracking nuts," he said.

"I'll never forget the time we used the fruitcake to play football," said Harriet.

"It almost hit your little brother," said George.
"That was a close call," said Harriet.
"Wow, fruitcake can be dangerous!"

"There is only one thing for us to do this Christmas," said Harriet.

"Avoid Ms. Hoozit and her fruitcake!" said George.

On Monday when Harriet and George
saw Ms. Hoozit shoveling,

they pulled down their hats
so she wouldn't recognize them.

On Tuesday when Harriet was helping
her dad put up Christmas lights,
Ms. Hoozit looked out her window.

So Harriet ducked behind a bush.

For the rest of the week,
Harriet and George hid from Ms. Hoozit.

BUS
STOP

By Friday, they were exhausted.
But it was worth it to avoid Ms. Hoozit's fruitcake.

On Christmas Eve, they saw Ms. Hoozit invite
Harriet's brother, Walt, in for a Christmas treat.

"Poor little pup," said George.
"Soon he'll be eating fruitcake," said Harriet.

When Walt finally came out of Ms. Hoozit's house
Harriet asked, "How was the fruitcake?"

YUMMY FUDGE

"Ms. Hoozit made fudge this year?" said George.

Before Walt could answer, Ms. Hoozit opened the door.
"Well, there you two are," she said.
"Come in for a Christmas treat."
"OK!" said Harriet.
"Fudge!" whispered George.

"I made a big batch of fudge this year!"
said Ms. Hoozit.
"Oh, boy!" said Harriet.
"But I could never find you two . . .

. . . and my fudge is all gone. But don't worry,
I still have a Christmas treat for you."

"Last year's fruitcake!
Eat up and Merry Christmas!" said Ms. Hoozit.